This book belongs to:

NICHOLE

THE ELEPHANT WHO LEARNED TO SHARE

by SUNNY GRIFFIN
ILLUSTRATED BY R.M. KOLDING

COPYRIGHT © 1993, LANDOLL
LANDOLL
Ashland, Ohio 44805

Edsel the elephant was very happy today
and his jungle friends all around
heard him say...

"From where do you suppose he came,
that smart little monkey with no name?

I'm so big and he was so very small.
His name he gave to me and didn't mind at all.

You could tell he
enjoyed giving, it's true.
I wonder if I gave away something,
would I feel good too?

Now just what is it I can afford to give?
In order to think, I'll have to go back
to where I live.

So good-bye friend Edgar and Eugene, too.
It's been so nice meeting both of you."

Edsel the elephant started out for home
down the narrow jungle path.

To figure out what I have to give, he thought,
I may have to learn some math.

The ivory tusks I have attached to my face...
aren't worth much to anyone in this place.

I'll have to think of something else to give away.
All of a sudden a little voice up above him did say...

"Come quickly and give of yourself to someone in need.
There is one right here in the jungle who could
use your help indeed."

Edsel looked up and
guess who he did see...
It was the no name monkey
and friends of three.

"Our blind friend Orville is
tangled up in a high green vine.
Not being able to see
gets him into trouble
all of the time.

Help us, oh please, to get him safely down...
with your trunk set him carefully
on the ground."

Now Edsel the elephant being very, very kind...

thought, This is the wealth I have to give at this time.

He only stopped for a
minute and then he said so sweet...
"I can do better than that, I will
become his four feet.

Why can't he always ride
on my broad grey back?
For there is nothing I can't do
or that he will lack.

On my ivory
tusks he can hang...
on my tail he can
boldly swing.

Up above he can safely
eat and soundly sleep...
when he's awake
from my ear to ear
he can leap.

With my eyes,
for him, I will see...
not far away from him
will I ever be."

When told, little Orville loved the idea
so much he bowed his head and cried.
He said, "I didn't know anyone cared if I lived or died.

Everyone has always been too busy to worry about me.
That's why I got in this predicament, can't you see!"

With a tear in his eye, Edsel hugged his new little friend.
They both agreed their friendship
would never end.

Gently holding little
Orville's tiny, frail frame...
Edsel turned to say
thanks to the monkey
with no name.

The monkeys were
nowhere to be seen...
but they knew what
this special friendship
would mean.

**Little blind Orville would always have someone to care...
and big grey Edsel's wealth of himself he would always share.**

Now there is one more thing
I would like to say...
"Do you know someone
you can help in any way?"